LAKE CLASSICS

Great American
Short Stories III

Henry
JAMES

Stories retold by Emily Hutchinson
Illustrated by James Balkovek

LAKE EDUCATION
Belmont, California

꧁꧂

LAKE CLASSICS

Great American Short Stories I

Washington Irving, Nathaniel Hawthorne, Mark Twain, Bret Harte, Edgar Allan Poe, Kate Chopin, Willa Cather, Sarah Orne Jewett, Sherwood Anderson, Charles W. Chesnutt

Great American Short Stories II

Herman Melville, Stephen Crane, Ambrose Bierce, Jack London, Edith Wharton, Charlotte Perkins Gilman, Frank R. Stockton, Hamlin Garland, O. Henry, Richard Harding Davis

Great American Short Stories III

Thomas Bailey Aldrich, Irvin S. Cobb, Rebecca Harding Davis, Theodore Dreiser, Alice Dunbar-Nelson, Edna Ferber, Mary Wilkins Freeman, Henry James, Ring Lardner, Wilbur Daniel Steele

Great British and Irish Short Stories

Arthur Conan Doyle, Saki (H. H. Munro), Rudyard Kipling, Katherine Mansfield, Thomas Hardy, E. M. Forster, Robert Louis Stevenson, H. G. Wells, John Galsworthy, James Joyce

Great Short Stories from Around the World

Guy de Maupassant, Anton Chekhov, Leo Tolstoy, Selma Lagerlöf, Alphonse Daudet, Mori Ogwai, Leopoldo Alas, Rabindranath Tagore, Fyodor Dostoevsky, Honoré de Balzac

Cover and Text Designer: Diann Abbott

Library of Congress Catalog Number: 95-76752
ISBN 1-56103-070-8
Printed in the United States of America
1 9 8 7 6 5 4 3 2 1

CONTENTS

❦ Lake Classic Short Stories ❧

> *"The universe is made of stories, not atoms."*
> —Muriel Rukeyser

> *"The story's about you."*
> —Horace

Everyone loves a good story. It is hard to think of a friendlier introduction to classic literature. For one thing, short stories are *short*—quick to get into and easy to finish. Of all the literary forms, the short story is the least intimidating and the most approachable.

Great literature is an important part of our human heritage. In the belief that this heritage belongs to everyone, *Lake Classic Short Stories* are adapted for today's readers. Lengthy sentences and paragraphs are shortened. Archaic words are replaced. Modern punctuation and spellings are used. Many of the longer stories are abridged. In all the stories,

5

painstaking care has been taken to preserve the author's unique voice.

Lake Classic Short Stories have something for everyone. The hundreds of stories in the collection cover a broad terrain of themes, story types, and styles. Literary merit was a deciding factor in story selection. But no story was included unless it was as enjoyable as it was instructive. And special priority was given to stories that shine light on the human condition.

Each book in the *Lake Classic Short Stories* is devoted to the work of a single author. Little-known stories of merit are included with famous old favorites. Taken as a whole, the collected authors and stories make up a rich and diverse sampler of the story-teller's art.

Lake Classic Short Stories guarantee a great reading experience. Readers who look for common interests, concerns, and experiences are sure to find them. Readers who bring their own gifts of perception and appreciation to the stories will be doubly rewarded.

🌿 Henry James 🌿
(1843–1916)

About the Author

Henry James came from a very distinguished American family. His grandfather was one of the first millionaires in America. His father was a philosopher. But even though the boy was surrounded by culture, he lived a rather lonely life in the family's New York mansion.

When James was just 12 years old, he was sent to Europe to study. He returned to America to enter Harvard Law School, but left after the first year. James had always shown a talent for writing. Now he began to write seriously.

From the time he was 26, James made Europe his home. Mostly he lived in England. Over time he became fascinated with the idea of the American in Europe. Many of his stories describe relationships between innocent and naive Americans and sophisticated, experienced Europeans. *Daisy Miller*, one of James's most famous novels, tells about the adventures of a young American woman abroad.

Because the James family had plenty of money, Henry was able to write what he pleased without worrying about public tastes. He took a great deal of time with his stories, carefully crafting each work. The "psychological story" became his trademark. In this kind of story, most of the action takes place in the thoughts and emotions of the characters.

In 1915, James became a subject of Great Britain. This was his show of support for Britain in World War I. He continued living there until his death the next year, in 1916.

James's later years are sometimes called his greatest period of writing. He was 60 when he published the famous story that follows, a tale called "The Beast in the Jungle."

The Beast in the Jungle

What's the worst fate you can imagine? The main character in this thoughtful story is quite certain that something *truly* important is in store for him. After a lifetime of waiting, he is amazed when he finally discovers what it was.

HE TRIED TO MAKE UP FOR HIS FAULTS BY INVITING
HIS FRIENDS TO THE OPERA.

The Beast in the Jungle

I

John Marcher and some friends had gone to visit the house where May Bartram was staying. As always, he felt lost in the crowd.

The house was called Weatherend. It was famous for its beauty and for all the fine things inside. There were wonderful pictures everywhere, heirlooms, and treasures of all the arts. Marcher and his friends had been invited for lunch. After lunch, the guests had moved off in all directions. Everyone wanted to tour the house, to admire the artwork.

There were so many rooms that guests could wander at their will. If they wanted to, they could stay back from the main group and look at things up close. All around, Marcher could see people bending toward art objects with their hands on their knees. They were nodding their heads as if their sense of smell had been excited. They reminded Marcher of dogs sniffing a cupboard.

John Marcher felt a bit annoyed by those people. They seemed to know *too* much about art. And he was annoyed just as much by those people who knew nothing. He needed to get away from the group for a moment. He wanted to better appreciate what he was seeing.

This led him, on that late October afternoon, to a closer meeting with May Bartram. He'd noticed her during lunch. They had sat at opposite ends of a long table. Right away he knew that he had seen her someplace before. But he couldn't quite remember where or when. Somehow he could tell that she had remembered him, too.

He had the feeling that her position in the house was as a poor relation. He also had the impression that she was not there on a brief visit. She seemed more or less a part of the household.

When May finally drifted toward him, he looked closely at her face. She was still an attractive woman, but no longer young. He could tell that she had suffered over the years.

By the time they spoke to each other, they were alone in one of the rooms. Their friends had just left and moved onto another part of the house. Without a word, they seemed to have agreed to stay behind for a talk. There was something of a charm between them.

As soon as he heard her voice, his memory came back to him. He almost jumped at it to get there before her.

"Why, I met you years and years ago in Rome," he said. "I remember it very clearly now."

She told him that she had been sure he'd forgotten about their meeting. So, to prove how well he remembered it, he began to tell her his memories. They seemed to pop up as he called for them. Marcher flattered himself that his memory was correct. Yet he was pleased when she smiled and corrected him.

In his hurry to make everything right, he had gotten most of the details wrong. Their meeting hadn't been in Rome, she reminded him—it had been in Naples. It hadn't been seven years before—it had been more like 10. And she hadn't been with her uncle and aunt, but with her mother and her brother.

She reminded him that he hadn't been with the Pembles, but with the Boyers. He had come with them from Rome. She was sure of that because she didn't know the Pembles. And it was the people he was with who had introduced them. Finally, the thunderstorm that had raged around them had not happened at the Palace of the Caesars, but at Pompeii.

Then, pretending a pout, May Bartram pointed out that he *really* didn't remember the least thing about her. He smiled at that, but now there didn't seem to be anything else to talk about. After all, it had not taken them long to say all they had to say. Unfortunately, the past could give them no more than it already had. They had met for the first time when she was 20 and he was 25.

Now they looked at each other as if an opportunity had been missed. The present moment would have been so much better if only the one in the past hadn't been so unimportant. Marcher said to himself that he ought to have done something worth remembering. If only he had saved her from a capsized boat in the bay! Or if he'd chased through the streets of Naples after a thief who'd snatched her purse. Or suppose he'd come down with a terrible fever, and she'd come in to look after him. *Then* at least they would have had something to talk about now.

It was useless to pretend that she was an old friend. Still, he wished that she was. He had enough new friends. At the other house, he was surrounded with them. If she had been a new friend, he probably wouldn't even have noticed her.

For a moment he thought of *inventing* something. Then she might make-believe with him that something romantic *had* happened. But he could think of nothing. They would separate soon, he knew. And this time there would be no second or third chance. They would have tried and not succeeded.

Just then, May herself decided to save the situation. He had felt that she was holding something back. She seemed to be hoping it wouldn't be necessary to bring it up. What she said, at any rate, quite cleared the air. It made him understand why he remembered her.

"You know, you told me something that I've never forgotten," she said. "Again and again, it has made me think of you. It was that very hot day when we went across the bay to Sorrento, for the breeze. You said it on the way back. We were sitting in the boat, enjoying the coolness. Have you forgotten?"

"I don't remember what I said," Marcher answered. "Yet I do remember that very hot day in Sorrento."

"I'm not so very sure you do," May Bartram said, with a small smile. "Yet the comment you made has remained with me. It was about yourself." She waited, as if it might come to him. But he gave no sign of remembering, so she went on. "Tell me, *has it ever happened?*"

He continued to stare at her. Then a light broke for him. The blood slowly came to his face. "Do you mean that I told you—?" But he stopped, afraid of saying anything more.

"It was something about yourself that one would never forget," she said. "That is, if one remembered you at all." She smiled. "That's why I ask you—did the thing you spoke of ever come to pass?"

Marcher was lost in wonder and embarrassment. He could see that she felt sorry for him. It was as if her question had been a mistake.

In the next moment, though, he knew that it had not been a mistake, but only a surprise. After the first shock of it, her secret knowledge seemed sweet to him.

She was the only other person in the world who would have that knowledge. And she'd had it all these years! He could hardly believe that he had breathed his secret and then forgotten about it! No wonder they couldn't have met as if nothing had happened.

"I remember our conversation now," he said. "I can hardly believe that I ever forgot it."

"Is it because you've told so many others as well?" she asked.

"But I've told *nobody* else. Not a single person since then."

"So I'm the only person who knows?"

"The only person in the world," he said.

"Well," she said quickly, "I myself have never spoken about it. I've never, never repeated what you told me that day. And I never will."

She spoke so sincerely that he believed her completely. "Please don't, then," he said, still embarrassed.

"Then you still feel the same way about it now?" she asked.

Now it was clear that she was truly

interested. For so long he had thought of himself as terribly alone. But now it seemed that he wasn't a bit alone. In fact, he hadn't been alone since those moments on the Sorrento boat. It was *she* who had been alone. To tell her what he had told her—why had he done it, but to ask something of her? And she had given it, without his having so much as thanked her. At first, what he'd asked of her had been simply not to laugh at him. For 10 years, she had beautifully not done so. And she was not doing so now.

"What *exactly* did I say to you?" he asked.

"Well, it was very simple. You said that, for as long as you could remember, you'd had a strong feeling inside. This feeling was that something rare and strange—perhaps even terrible—would happen to you sooner or later. You had the feeling deep in your bones that this thing might even overwhelm you."

"Do you call that 'very simple'?" John Marcher asked.

She thought for a moment. "What I

meant was—I seemed to understand it as you spoke."

"You *do* understand it?" he asked eagerly.

She looked closely at him with kind eyes. "You still have that belief, then?"

There was too much to say, so Marcher said nothing.

"So, whatever it is, it hasn't yet come," she asked.

He shook his head. "It hasn't yet come. Only, you know, it isn't that I have to *do* anything. It's not anything I'm to achieve in the world, or to be admired for."

"I see," she said. "It's to be something you will be asked to suffer."

"Well, say to *wait for*. It's something I have to meet, to face, to see suddenly happen in my life. I feel that it will possibly destroy me. Or it might just change everything, striking at the root of all my world."

She took this in. "Perhaps what you describe is just the danger—familiar to so many people—of falling in love?"

John Marcher thought about that. "Did

you ask me that before?"

"No. I wasn't so free and easy then. But it's what strikes me now."

"Of course," he said after a moment. "What's in store for me may be no more than that. But if it had been that, I would know by now."

"What do you mean? Because you've already been in love?" she asked.

"Yes. I've been in love. And it hasn't been overwhelming."

"Ah! Then it hasn't been love," said May Bartram.

"Well, at least I *thought* it was. I took it for that. It was agreeable. It was delightful. It was miserable. But it wasn't strange. It wasn't what *my* fate is to be."

"You want something all to yourself," she said. "You want something that nobody else knows or *has* known?"

"It isn't a question of what I *want*. It's only a question of the feeling that haunts me. I live with this feeling every day."

"Do you have a sense of coming violence?" she asked him.

"I don't think of it as violent. I only think of it as natural. And above all, unmistakable. I think of it simply as *the* thing. *The* thing will of itself appear natural."

"Then how will it appear strange?"

Marcher thought for a moment. "It won't—to *me*."

"To whom then?"

"Well," he said, smiling, "perhaps it will seem strange to you."

"Oh, then, *I'm* to be present?"

"Why, May, you *are* present—since you know about it."

"I see." She turned it over in her mind. "But I mean at the time of the event."

Then the mood between them became more serious. "It will depend on you—on whether you'll watch with me," he said.

"Are you afraid?" she asked.

"Don't leave me *now*," he went on.

"Are you afraid?" she repeated.

"Do you think I'm out of my mind?" he said, instead of answering directly.

"No, I don't," said May Bartram. "I understand you. I believe you."

"Then you *will* watch with me?"

She hesitated. Then she asked again, "Are you afraid?"

"If you'll watch with me, you'll see."

"Very well, then," she said. By this time, they had moved across the room. At the door, they paused.

"I'll watch with you," said May Bartram.

II

The fact that she "knew" began to create a bond between them. During the next year, they met several times again. Marcher had paid another visit to the friends who liked to visit Weatherend. These friends had taken him back there. He had talked with Miss Bartram then.

Once or twice Miss Bartram had gone with her great aunt to London. There, Marcher had persuaded her to take a few brief absences from her aunt. At those times, they went together to various art galleries and museums. They talked about Italy. In short, they became good friends. Toward the end of that year, May Bartram's great aunt died. The terms of her aunt's will allowed Miss Bartram to set up a small home in London. She and John Marcher now lived in the same city. That fact made it easier for their friendship to grow.

He was careful to remember that she had a life of her own. There were things that might happen to *her*. He had always thought of himself as an unselfish person. That was the real reason, in fact, why marriage was out of the question.

His belief, his fear, his obsession, was not something he could ask a woman to share. Something or other lay in wait for him. He *knew* that. In the twists and turns of the years, it lay like a crouching beast in the jungle.

It didn't matter whether the crouching beast would kill him or be killed. The point was that it *would* spring on him one day. And a man of feeling didn't bring a lady along on a tiger hunt. How could he ever marry?

As time went by, Marcher was to find

out that May was all the while looking at his life. She was judging it in the light of his secret. It was never mentioned between them except as "the real truth" about him. That had always been what he called it. Now she began to use the term, too.

She had a wonderful way of making it seem the secret of her own life, too. Above all, only she knew the truth about the difference between his outer appearance and his true feelings.

Marcher went through the motions of doing his job. He took care of his garden and his home. He accepted and repaid social invitations of the people he knew in London. Only May Bartram knew that he wore a social mask for the world. By some wonderful trick, it seemed that she, too, could look out the eyes of that mask. It was as if she were looking over his shoulder.

So, while they grew old together, she watched with him. She let their friendship give shape and color to her own life. There were long periods when a stranger might have listened to them and found nothing worth listening to. On the other hand, the real truth might rise to the surface at any time. Then indeed the listener would have wondered what they were talking about.

"What saves us, you know, is that we *appear* to be so normal. We look like a man and woman whose friendship has become a daily habit." She made this remark quite often. But one afternoon, it took a different turn. He had come to visit her in honor of her birthday. This event had fallen on a Sunday, in a season of thick fog and general gloom.

He had brought her his usual offering. By now he knew her so well that a hundred little customs had been established. It was one of his proofs to himself, this present he gave her on her birthday. It showed him that he had not sunk into real selfishness. Usually he gave her nothing more than a small object. But it was always the best of its kind. He was always careful to pay more than he thought he could afford for it.

"Our habit saves you, don't you see?" she said, with a twinkle in her eye. "It makes you just like other men. So many men spend endless time with dull women. *I'm* your dull woman—a part of the daily bread for which you pray at church. That covers your tracks more than anything."

"And what covers yours?" asked Marcher, smiling. "I see, of course, what you mean by saving *me*. At least as far as other people are concerned. Ah yes, I've seen that all along. But what is it that saves *you*? I often wonder about that, you know."

"Where other people are concerned, you mean?" she asked.

"I sometimes ask myself if it's quite fair. Fair, I mean, to have taken up all your time," he said. "I almost feel as if you hadn't really had the time to do anything else."

"Anything else but be interested?" she asked. "Ah, but what else is important? If I've been 'watching' with you, it has always been interesting."

"Oh, certainly," John Marcher said. "But doesn't it sometimes seem that your curiosity is not being repaid?"

May Bartram paused. "Do you ask that because yours *isn't*? I mean, because you have had to wait so long?"

He understood what she meant. "Waiting for the thing to happen that never does happen? For the beast to jump out? No. It isn't a matter I can choose. It's in the lap of the gods."

"Yes," Miss Bartram replied. "Of course, one's fate is always coming. Of course, it *has* come, in its own form and its own way, all the while. Only, you know, *yours* was to have been something special."

Something in her words made him look at her with suspicion. "You say 'was to have been,' as if in your heart, you had begun to doubt."

"Oh!" she said.

"As if you thought that it's too late and nothing will now take place."

She shook her head slowly. "Oh, no. You're wrong about that."

He continued to look at her. "What then is the matter with you?"

"Well," she said, "there is only one thing the matter with me. And it's this: I'm more sure than ever that my curiosity, as you call it, will be *too* well repaid."

They were serious now. He got up and walked about her little drawing room. Every object in it was as familiar to him as the things of his own house. The very carpets were worn with his fitful walk. The years of his nervous moods had been at work there. In a way, the place was the written history of his whole middle life. "Is it possible that you've grown afraid?" he asked.

"Afraid?" she asked. As she repeated the word, he saw that his question had made her change color.

Then he said, "You remember asking *me* that same question long ago—that first day at Weatherend?"

"Oh, yes, and you told me you didn't know. You said that I was to see for myself. Well, we've said little about it to each other since then, have we? Even in so long a time."

"Exactly," Marcher said. "It's almost as if we thought we might find out that I *am* afraid. Then we wouldn't quite know what to do, would we?"

She had no answer to this question. "There have been days when I thought you were," May said.

"I hope, however, that you see I'm not afraid now," Marcher answered.

"What I see is that you've gotten used to danger. Living with it so long and so closely, you've lost your sense of it. You know it's there, but you don't care. I don't think anyone could have a better attitude."

John Marcher smiled. "It's heroic?"

"Certainly—call it that."

"I *am*, then, a man of courage?"

"That's what you have shown me."

Yet he still wondered. "But doesn't a true man of courage know what he's afraid of—or *not* afraid of? I don't know that, you know. I can't name it."

"But it isn't the end of our watch, is it,

John? Surely it isn't the end of *yours*. You still have everything to see."

All that day he had the feeling that she was keeping something back. He still had that feeling now. "Perhaps you know something I don't," he said. Then his voice trembled a little. "Somehow you know what's going to happen," he said, trying to hold on to the picture of himself as a man of courage.

Her silence was almost a confession. And so was the look on her face. Now he was sure. "You *know*—and you're afraid to tell me. It's so bad that you're afraid I'll find out."

She looked as if he'd crossed some invisible line that she'd secretly drawn around herself. But she had nothing to worry about, and neither did he.

"You'll never find out," she said.

III

Marcher had always tried his best not to be selfish. If he ever thought he'd been selfish, he would quickly tip the scales the other way. Often he would try to make up for his faults by inviting his friend to go with him to the opera. Sometimes they would go quite often. After the opera they would eat dinner together in May's home. Then they might play a few passages of the opera together, on her piano.

On one of these evenings, Marcher reminded her that she'd never answered the question he'd asked on her last birthday. "Tell me, May. What is it that saves *you*?" he asked again.

He was asking, of course, how she "saved" herself from the gossips. Most women her age were married. He wondered how she avoided being talked about. Society gossips could be very cruel to people who were different from themselves in any way.

"I never said that I wasn't talked about," May Bartram replied.

"Ah, well then, you're *not* 'saved.'"

"It has not been an important question for me. If you've had your woman, I've had my man," she said.

"And you mean that makes you all right?"

"I don't see why it shouldn't make me as right as it makes you."

"I see," said Marcher. "Our friendship shows that you're living for something. Not, that is, just for me and my secret."

May Bartram smiled. "I don't pretend that it shows I'm not living for you. It's my closeness with you that's in question."

He laughed as he saw what she meant. "Yes, I see. You help me to pass for a man like any other. So if *I* am, then you can pass as being ordinary, too."

"That's it," she said. "It's all that concerns me—to help you pass for a man like any other."

"How kind, how beautiful, you are to me! How shall I ever repay you?"

"By going on as you are," she said quietly.

So they went on in the same way for several years. Oddly enough, he began to feel something that he had never felt before. He felt a fear that he might lose her through some terrible catastrophe.

It wouldn't be *the* catastrophe, though. There was a reason he had this awful feeling. He began to notice that her health was failing.

One day, May Bartram told him that something serious was wrong with her blood. He immediately began to imagine the worst. "What if she were to die before knowing, before seeing—?" he wondered. On the other hand, what if she knew something already? This would make the whole thing even worse. His curiosity about his own life had become the basis of her life. She had been living to see what would happen to him. It would be cruel to her to have to give up before finding out.

Because of her illness, she hardly ever left the house now. Instead of meeting her somewhere in London, he had to go to her house to see her. He found her always seated by her fire. She'd be laid back in the deep, old-fashioned chair that she was less and less able to leave.

One day, he was suddenly struck by the fact that she looked old. Then he realized that only his awareness was sudden. After so many years, she looked older because she really *was* old, or coming to be old anyway.

Naturally, this was even more true of himself. If *she* was old, or almost, John Marcher *surely* was. This dawning awareness brought the truth home to him. His surprises began here. And when they had once begun, they multiplied, coming in a rush. It was as if they were *meant* to be kept back until the late afternoon of his life.

He began to wonder if his big fate was just this. Was it to be that he would see this charming woman, this good friend, pass away from him? If this was it, it certainly seemed a big letdown. It would mean that his entire life had been the most terrible of failures.

Marcher felt sick. He had never thought of his life as a failure before. Always he had been waiting for the appearance that was to make it a success. But he had waited for quite a different thing—not for this.

Then he recognized that *she* had waited almost as long as he had. Had she been waiting in vain? This idea affected him sharply. He became even more upset as she became more and more ill. What did it all mean? What, that is, did *she* mean? Had his faithful friend waited all her life for nothing?

And what about him? Was *nothing* to happen to him? It wouldn't have been such a failure to be poor, to have lost his good name, or even to be hanged. The worst failure was not to *be* anything. He was not too old to suffer. If only he could suffer enough to make up for the long wait. Now he had only one desire left— that his wait would not end without anything having happened.

IV

One afternoon, in early spring, he went to see her. For the first time that year, May Bartram sat without a fire. For some reason, Marcher had the feeling that she would never see a fire again.

The look on her own face—he could hardly have said why—made that feeling even stronger.

Her face was almost as white as wax. It was covered with fine lines. She wore a faded green scarf. In Marcher's mind, she was the picture of a peaceful but mysterious sphinx. Yet more than a statue, with her white petals and green fronds, she might have been a lily, too.

She seemed that day to be on the other side of some gulf. He felt she had already left him. Was it because she knew the answer to their question? Was it because her work, then, was already done?

He remembered that he'd asked her about this a few months before. Even then he'd thought that she knew something and was keeping it from him. Finally he asked her, "Please tell me something. What do you think is the very worst thing that can happen to me?"

In the past, he had asked her that question often enough. They had spoken about terrible things that *might* happen. Now she looked at him for a long moment before speaking. He looked into her eyes. They still seemed as beautiful as they had been in her youth. Only now, they were beautiful with a strange, cold light. Before she could answer him, he said, "You know something that I don't. You've shown me that before."

She said firmly, "I've shown you, my dear, nothing."

He shook his head. "You can't hide it. You admitted it months ago. I said it was something you were afraid I would find out. Your answer was that I couldn't, that I wouldn't. I don't pretend that I have. But you had something in mind. I see now what it must be. It's the worst thing that could happen. This is why I *insist* that you tell me. I'm only afraid of ignorance now. I'm not afraid of knowledge."

After a long silence, she spoke. "It *would* be the worst. I mean the thing that I've never said."

It hushed him for a moment. "Worse than anything we've ever imagined?"

"Much worse."

Marcher thought. "You *must* tell me what you know. Otherwise, you will be leaving me all alone."

"No, no!" she said. "I'm with you—don't you see?—still." As if to make it clear to him, she rose from her chair. It was something she seldom did these days. "I haven't left you."

He knew how hard it was for her to stand up. So her action meant a great deal to him. He could see that she was still able to help him. But at the same time, it seemed that at any instant her light might go out. So he decided to make the most of it. He thought of three or four questions he wanted to ask. Finally he asked what he thought was the most important. "Then tell me if I shall consciously suffer."

She shook her head. "Never!"

"Well, what's better than that? Do you call that the worst?"

"You think there could be nothing better?" she asked.

As their eyes met, he gasped. An idea came to him that suddenly made everything seem clear. "I see—if I don't suffer!"

Her own look was full of doubt. "You see what?"

"Why, I think I see what you mean—what you've always meant."

She shook her head. "What I mean isn't what I've always meant. It's different."

"It's something new?"

"Yes," she said. "Something new. It's not what you think. I see what you think."

"It isn't that it's all a mistake?" he asked.

"A mistake?" she echoed. *That* possibility would truly be terrible. "Oh, no. It's nothing like that. You've been right all along."

"Are you telling me the truth? I haven't been waiting just to see the door shut in my face?"

She shook her head again. "Whatever it is, it *is* something. The door isn't shut. The door is open," said May Bartram.

"Then something is to come?"

"It's never too late," she said. She had

walked closer to him. He had been standing by the mantel. Now her hand grasped the shelf, as if for support. He felt that she had something more to tell him. She stood close, her face shining at him. For a moment they looked at each other silently. He waited for her to say something more, but she didn't.

Something else took place instead. It began with the simple closing of her eyes. At the same instant, she gave way to a slow, fine shudder. Then she turned and went back to her chair.

"Well—?" he asked.

She had touched a servant's bell near the mantel. Then she had sunk back, strangely pale. "I'm afraid I'm too ill."

"Too ill to tell me?" He began to fear that she would die without giving him any more information.

"Oh, John, don't you know—now?" she whispered.

She spoke as if something important had happened. But her maid, answering the bell, was already in the room with them.

"I know nothing," he said.

"Oh!" said May Bartram.

"Are you in pain?" he asked, as her maid went to her.

"No," said May Bartram.

Her maid gave him a look that said otherwise. In spite of that, he asked, "What then has happened?"

With the maid's help, she was once more on her feet. He had found his hat and gloves and had reached the door. Yet he waited for her answer.

"What *was* to have happened," she said mysteriously.

V

When he came back the next day, she was not able to see him. In all the time he had known her, this had never happened before. Now he turned away, almost angry. He felt that this really might be the beginning of the end. She was dying, and he would lose her. She was dying, and his life would end. On his way home he stopped in the park. Soon he became lost in thought.

To save him, she had lied to him. What could his fate be, but this? It was this thing that had just begun to happen. Her dying, her death, his loneliness after that. That was the beast in the jungle. That was what had been in the lap of the gods. He'd had her word for it as he left her. What else could she have meant?

He saw it all now. His fate was not to be a rare and overwhelming thing. It was no more than a common doom. But at this hour, poor Marcher felt that the common doom was enough. This was his fate, and he would accept it. He sat down on a bench in the twilight. He had lived with her help. To leave her behind now would be to miss her terribly. What could be more overwhelming than that?

Well, he was to know within the week. She finally received him where she had always received him. Once he was seated by her chair, she said, "Dear John, I'm not sure you understood. You have nothing to wait for now. It *has* come."

Oh, how he looked at her! *"Really?"*

"Really."

"The thing that, as you said, *was* to?"

"The thing that we began in our youth to watch for."

Face to face with her once more, he believed her. "It has come in the night then? Come and passed me by?"

May Bartram wore her strange, faint smile. "Oh, no, it hasn't passed you by!"

"But if I didn't notice it, and it hasn't touched me—?"

"Ah, the fact that you didn't notice it is the strangeness in the strangeness. It's the wonder *of* the wonder." She spoke with confidence. "It *has* touched you. It has made you all its own."

"But without my knowing it?"

"Yes. It's enough if *I* know it. What I said long ago is true. You'll never know now, but even at that I think you should be happy. You've *had* it," said May Bartram.

"But had what?" he asked.

"Well, the thing that was to have made you different," she said. "It has acted. I'm glad to have been able to see what it's *not*. What was to happen *has* happened, don't you see? It is all over now. It's past. It's behind us now."

It came to him that he was standing before her for the last time. Knowing that was a weight he could not bear. Yet he continued to talk about it.

"I believe you," he said. "But I can't begin to pretend that I understand. *Nothing* for me is past. How can the thing I've never felt at all be the thing I was marked out to feel?"

"You take your feelings too much for granted," she said. "You were to *suffer* your fate. That doesn't mean that you were to *know* it."

"How can that be? Such suffering and the knowledge of it go together."

She looked at him for a few minutes before speaking again. "No—you don't understand."

"I suffer," said John Marcher.

"Don't, don't!"

"How can I help at least *that*?"

"*Don't!*" May Bartram repeated.

She spoke in such a tone that he stared

at her. A strange light seemed to shimmer across his vision. "Do you mean that I haven't the right—? Is it because of that, then, you're dying?" he asked.

She watched him closely for a moment—as if she were looking for something. "I would live for you still—if I could. But I can't!" she said.

She couldn't indeed. They had parted forever in that strange talk. Over the next few weeks, he was not allowed to come into her room of pain. The doctors, nurses, and the few relatives who came by had more rights than he had. Even the stupidest fourth cousin had more rights to see her than he did.

There were not many people at her funeral. But he was treated as if he were one person among a thousand. He had somehow not expected this. The family did not even recognize him as a man who was in mourning for her, which, of course, he was.

With May Bartram gone, John Marcher became an entirely different man. The change from his old life to his new life was complete and final. What was to happen *had* happened in such a way that he had neither fear nor hope about his own future. It was in this spirit that he decided to travel.

He started on a journey that was to be as long as he could make it. However, before he left London he made a visit to May Bartram's grave. He stood there for an hour, unable to turn away. He looked at her name and the dates on her gravestone. He waited, as if some message would rise up to him. But her two names on the stone were like a pair of eyes that didn't know him. He gave them a lost long look, but no light broke.

VI

He stayed away from England for a year. He visited many beautiful places in Asia. But no matter what wonders he saw, they all seemed vulgar and vain. He remembered his time with May Bartram as a light that had colored and refined his life. Compared to that light, the glow of the East was cheap and thin.

As he stood before the tombs of kings, he would often think about her small grave in London. For him, that had become the one proof of his own past glory. It wasn't surprising that he came back to it the morning he returned to London. As he stood there, he felt that he was near the only part of himself that he valued.

The person beneath the earth *knew* of his rare experience. The plot of ground, the gravestone, and the flowers seemed to *belong* to him. For an hour, he felt like a happy landlord looking at a piece of his own property. He made up his mind that he would never again travel far from this spot. He would come back to it every month.

In the oddest way, May Bartram's grave soon became for him a place of happiness. This garden of death was the few square feet of earth on which he was most alive.

Standing there, he felt as if he had his hand through the arm of a companion.

In a strange way, that companion was his other, younger self. He felt as if he and his companion were wandering around and around a third person. He also felt that the third person *watched*—her eyes never ceasing to follow him.

This went on for a year. It would probably have gone on even longer, but one day something happened. It was a simple thing of chance. He happened to look at the face of another man. This face looked into Marcher's own with a look like the cut of a blade. Marcher felt it so deep down that he winced at the pain.

The man had been standing at a nearby grave. Since that grave seemed to be fresh, Marcher knew that the emotion of the visitor was new. As Marcher stood at May Bartram's grave, he had become aware of his neighbor, a middle-aged man, dressed in mourning. He saw only the man's bowed back.

Marcher was involved in his own sadness that day. He was thinking that he had nothing to live for. He felt like stretching himself out on May Bartram's grave. It seemed, for the moment, like the perfect place to receive his last sleep. What in all the wide world did he have now to keep awake for?

As he was thinking these mournful thoughts, he was shocked at the look of the other man's face.

Having just left the new grave, the man was walking along the path toward one of the gates. This brought him closer to Marcher. The man was walking so slowly that for a minute the two men were looking straight at each other. Marcher could see that the other man was deeply stricken with grief. It was the only thing anyone would notice about him. The look on his face was a study in sorrow.

As the man passed, Marcher wondered in pity about the man's sadness. What had he *had* that could cause him such sorrow when he lost it?

It was something—and this hit him with a pang—that he, John Marcher, had not had. The proof was in John Marcher's own feelings. No passion had ever touched him, really. He had survived and wandered and cried a little. But where had *his* deep pain been?

The sight that had just met his eyes made him see something that he had completely missed before. He had missed real life and love. He had lived *outside* of his life. He had not felt it within.

The way a woman was mourned when she had been loved for herself—that was the look on the man's face. The knowledge came to Marcher all of a sudden. He finally understood how empty his life had been. Now at last he knew that *she* was what he had missed.

This was the awful thought—the answer to all the past. It made his heart turn as cold as the stone beneath him. Now everything fell together at once, overwhelming him. He realized how blind he had been.

The fate that was waiting for him was now clear. He had been the man to whom nothing on earth was to have happened. *That* was the rare stroke. That was what was unusual about him. Now, in pale horror, he saw it all quite clearly.

So *she* had seen it, while he didn't! The truth was that all the time he was waiting, the wait was to be his life. At a certain moment, May Bartram had understood this. And she had offered him the chance to escape his fate. But all he had done was to just stare stupidly at the escape she was offering him.

The escape would have been to love her. Then, *then*—he would have lived. She had lived, simply by loving him for himself. But he had never seen her except in the ways that she had become of some use to him.

Now her words came back to him. The beast had been there indeed, and it had sprung. It had sprung in the twilight of that cold April when she stood up from her chair. Pale, ill, wasted, but beautiful, she had stood before him to let him guess. When he failed to guess, as she hopelessly turned from him, the beast had sprung.

Marcher had failed in everything he was fated to fail in. A moan now rose to his lips as he remembered how she had not wanted him to suffer. This horror of knowing the truth brought tears to his eyes. He tried to hold on to the horror so that he might feel the pain. The pain, at least, had something of the taste of life.

But the bitterness of it all suddenly sickened him as he understood what his life had been. He saw the Jungle of his life, and he saw the lurking Beast. Now he imagined the Beast rising, huge and ugly, to leap on him. To avoid it, he flung himself face down on the tomb.

The Two Faces

Just how far will a jealous woman go to get revenge? Lord Gwyther and Mrs. Grantham were once in love. Now he wants her to do a favor for his pretty young wife! How does she react? Read on to find out.

TEA AT BURBECK WAS A BRILLIANT SCENE. IT WAS
ALWAYS SERVED ON THE TERRACE.

The Two Faces

I

The servant continued to stand there after announcing the guest. This was not normal—but he seemed to have his reasons.

Mrs. Grantham repeated the name. "Lord Gwyther?" she asked, quickly looking at her companion. He was a short, fair young man. He was clean-shaven and had sharp eyes. Now he jumped to his feet and moved over to the fireplace. Mrs. Grantham stayed in her chair. "Well, Bates?" she said to the servant. "Where is he?"

"Shall I show him up, ma'am?" asked the servant.

"But of course!" she answered.

When she realized why the servant was not sure about this, she became a little annoyed. As Bates left the room, Mrs. Grantham turned to the young man. "Why in the world not—? What a way—!" she exclaimed.

"He wasn't sure that you'd see anyone," said Sutton, her gentleman friend.

"Well, I don't see *anyone*. I see individuals," she answered.

"That's just it—and sometimes you don't see even them," Sutton said.

"Do you mean because of *you*?" she asked. She moved a ringlet of hair back into place. "That's none of Bates's business. I shall speak to him about it."

"Don't," said young Sutton. "It's best to never notice anything."

"That's nice advice coming from you," she laughed. "You notice everything!"

"Ah, but I *say* nothing," he answered.

She looked at him for a moment. "Don't go anywhere."

"Really? I must sit him out?" he asked. He watched Mrs. Grantham as she glanced in the mirror. He could tell that her feelings were stronger than she thought she could hide. "If you're wondering how you look, I can tell you," he said. "Very cool and easy-going."

She looked at him carefully. "And if you're wondering how *you* look—"

"Oh, I'm not!" he laughed. "I always know. And you're looking lovely, within your own limits, of course. But that's enough. Don't try to be clever and witty."

"Then who *will* be?" she asked, with a little frown.

"There you are!" he laughed.

"Do you know him?" she asked as they heard footsteps in the hall.

Sutton had to think for a minute. Then he said "No," just as Lord Gwyther was announced again.

Lord Gwyther was a young man, stout and smooth and fresh. He was not at all shy, though. After he said hello to her, he put out his hand to her companion. "How do you do?" he said.

"Mr. Shirley Sutton," Mrs. Grantham said, introducing her friend.

For the next 20 minutes, all sorts of things occurred to Sutton. He saw that it would certainly *not* be better if he left. For some reason Mrs. Grantham seemed a little tense. And besides, Sutton wanted to stay and hear the whole conversation. This was especially true after Lord Gwyther announced that he was now married. And not only that, but he wanted to bring his wife to meet Mrs. Grantham.

Mrs. Grantham smiled, but it seemed to be a serious smile. "I think, you know, that you should have told me about your marriage before this," she said.

Sutton was certain that she had known about the marriage for some time, just as everyone else did.

"Do you mean when I first got engaged?" Lord Gwyther said. "Well, it took place so far away. We really told very few people at home."

Mrs. Grantham thought there might have been other reasons for not telling her. Still, it had not been quite right to keep it from her. "You were married in Germany?" she said. "That wasn't really so far away, you know. I would have been delighted to be there."

"Awfully kind of you," Lord Gwyther answered. "But of course, everyone knows that you *would* be kind. It wasn't in a big city in Germany, though. It was way out in the country. We *would* have had the wedding in England. But her mother, of course, wanted to be there. And her health wasn't good enough for her to travel. So you see, it was really a very small wedding."

"Will she be, then, a German?" Mrs. Grantham went on.

Sutton hid a little smile. Of course Mrs. Grantham already knew very well what Lady Gwyther "would be."

"Oh, dear, no!" said Lord Gwyther. "My father-in-law is proud to be British. But his wife, you see, has property in Germany. This property came from *her* mother. They've lived there for many years. So although Valda was born at home, she has spent most of her life over there."

"Oh, I see," said Mrs. Grantham. "Is Valda her name, then?"

"Well, like her mother, she has about 13 names," the young man said. "But Valda is the one we generally use."

Mrs. Grantham waited but an instant. "Then may *I* generally use it?"

"It would be too charming of you. Nothing would please us more," said Lord Gwyther.

"Then I think instead of you coming alone, you might have brought her to see me," said Mrs. Grantham.

"That's what I came to ask you," he said quickly. "I was hoping it would be all right."

He explained that for the moment Lady Gwyther was not in town. She was away, visiting some relatives. She had seen no one in London yet. And no one— not that it mattered—had seen her. She knew nothing about the ways of high society and was very frightened about facing it. The poor girl was not sure what might be expected of her.

"She wants someone who knows the whole thing, don't you see?" he said. Then he went on. "Someone who is very kind and clever—as you are, if I may say so—to take her by the hand."

When Lord Gwyther said this, Mrs. Grantham's eyes met Mr. Sutter's. But Lord Gwyther didn't seem to notice.

"She needs, if I may tell you so, a real friend to help her," he went on. "I asked myself what I could do to make things easier for her. I tried to think of who would be *absolutely* the best woman in London—"

"You thought naturally of *me*?" Mrs. Grantham asked.

This brought Shirley Sutton, looking at his watch, immediately to his feet.

"She is the best woman in London!" he said. Then he offered his hand in farewell to their hostess.

"You're not going?" asked Mrs. Grantham.

"I must," he said.

"Do we meet at dinner then?" she

asked, looking closely at him.

"I hope so," Sutton said with a smile. Then he returned to Lord Gwyther the friendly handshake he had received earlier.

II

Sutton and Mrs. Grantham did meet at dinner. As it happened, they did not sit side by side. But later they sat in a corner of the drawing room to have a private talk.

All afternoon Shirley Sutton had been thinking about Mrs. Grantham's face. He was remembering how it had changed during Lord Gwyther's visit. Something new had quickly come into it. He couldn't as yet have said what. In fact, he didn't even know if the change was for the better or for the worse. Until he figured it out, he would say nothing.

All he knew was that the situation had suddenly turned very exciting. He was afraid that the excitement would be contagious. That's why he had left, even though she had asked him not to. He was afraid he might say something that was not quite proper.

Now, in the drawing room, they could talk freely. In various corners, other couples were doing the same thing. Sutton was aware that his interest in Mrs. Grantham was known to their social set. He also knew London very well. He knew that he was on the way to being seen by people as Lord Gwyther's replacement. Everyone was quite angry with Lord Gwyther for the way he had treated Mrs. Grantham. In fact, they thought that his lordship had no right to suddenly become engaged and then so quickly married.

"I thought that you'd want me to leave," Shirley Sutton said. "I was sure you hadn't guessed—"

"That he would have dared to make such a strange request? No, of course I hadn't guessed. Who *would*? In any case," she said, "I told him I would help his wife. He wants me to get her ready to be introduced to all our friends."

"And you'll really and truly help her?"

"Really and truly?" Mrs. Grantham said with a little smile. "Why not? For what do you take me?"

"Ah, isn't that just what I ask myself every day?" said Shirley Sutton with a look of affection.

She had stood up. As he stood too, he said, "If you *do* help her, you know, you'll show him you've understood."

"Understood what?"

"Why, his idea, as one may say, to take the bull by the horns. In any case, he would have to be afraid that you might act against her. This way, he plays the wise game, you see. He treats your goodwill as a real thing. And he publicly places himself under an obligation to you."

"What do you mean when you say I would act against her?" she asked.

Sutton did not answer the question. Instead he said, "He takes his risk. But, you see, he puts you on your honor."

She thought for a moment more. "Well, you'll see what my honor can be depended on to do." Then she moved away, leaving Sutton standing there alone.

III

Shirley Sutton and Mrs. Grantham didn't meet again until the great party at Burbeck. This party was to be a gathering of 30 people. It was to go on from a certain Friday to the following Monday. Sutton arrived on Friday evening.

Mrs. Grantham had not yet arrived. Sutton found out that she would be coming on Saturday with a small group. He got this information from Miss Banker, who always knew all the gossip. She was like a big book that opened itself at the right place. For Sutton, she opened at the letter G—, which happened to be exactly right. "She's waiting to bring Lady Gwyther along with her."

"Ah, the Gwythers are coming?" he asked.

"Yes. *She'll* be the feature, of course.

Everyone wants to see her," said Miss Banker. "Poor little Lady Gwyther has just arrived in England. Now she will appear for the first time in her life in any society whatever. And isn't it just wonderful that Mrs. Grantham is helping her? It's just as if Mrs. Grantham were actually 'presenting' her. It's all so *interesting*, don't you think? Especially after Lord Gwyther threw her over. It wasn't so much the fact that he did it, but the *way* he did it that was so bad!"

Sutton seemed to wonder. "Oh? What was so terrible about the way he did it?"

"Why, he simply went and *did* it—took to himself this child," Miss Banker said in an excited whisper. "He did it without even breaking it off with Mrs. Grantham first. It happened before she could even turn around!"

"I follow you," he said. "But it would appear from what you say that she *has* turned around now."

"Well," Miss Banker laughed, "we shall soon see. That's what *everyone* will be trying to see."

"Oh, then, we have our work cut out!" said Sutton.

The next day, Sutton took a little stroll on the grounds with Miss Banker. He spoke as one who had done some further thinking about their talk.

"Did I understand from you yesterday that Lady Gwyther is a 'child'?"

"Nobody knows. Mrs. Grantham has kept her quite hidden. We'll see Lady Gwyther at tea today. I have a rather creepy feeling about it."

"Creepy?" asked Sutton.

"Yes. Because so much depends on the first impression. It seems to me that we're all here very much as the Roman mob at the circus used to be. We, like they, are waiting to see the next Christian brought out to the tigers."

"An interesting picture," said Sutton. "Do you really think so?"

"Oh, yes. Mrs. Grantham will have prepared her—decked her out for the sacrifice with ribbons and flowers."

"Ah, you mean that she'll have taken Lady Gwyther to the dressmaker!" said

Sutton. It came to him that this, perhaps, was all poor Lord Gwyther might have been asking of their friend. It simply could be that he didn't trust his wife's taste in clothes. Perhaps the styles in Germany were very different from those in England.

Tea at Burbeck was always served, weather permitting, on a shaded stretch of the terrace. Shirley Sutton had been wandering around the grounds when he came upon the place. He looked around and saw the linen-topped tables and glittering plates. There were rugs and cushions and ices and fruit and dozens of beautiful women. It was a brilliant scene—almost like grand opera. His imagination was stirred. One of the beautiful women might rise with a gold cup and sing a dramatic love song!

As it happened, one of them did rise as Sutton drew near. It was Mrs. Grantham, walking toward him. The two of them met on the terrace, away from the others. He saw that she was on her way into the house on some errand. It seemed that she wanted to get something or call someone. They met, in fact, by accident.

It struck him that she felt herself to be the most important person there. Her looks were perfect. Her very beauty looked out at him. But as their eyes met, he found himself looking at something else. Something had changed in her, but he couldn't tell just what.

He looked around for Lady Gwyther, but she was not there. He saw, though, that Mrs. Grantham knew what he was looking for. Why did this cause her expression to become hard and sharp, especially when she was looking so beautiful? A feeling of anxiety and suspense came over him. He realized now that he really cared how Mrs. Grantham would behave toward Lady Gwyther. And he knew that he wouldn't wait long to find out. Something was certainly in the air that would tell him.

What was in the air came down to earth the next moment. He turned around as he saw Mrs. Grantham watching someone coming toward them. A little person, very young and very much dressed, had come out of the house. The look in Mrs. Grantham's eyes was that of the artist admiring her work. The little person drew nearer. Without looking at him, Sutton's companion gave the small person a name. "Valda!" she called out.

Then he saw many things—too many. They appeared to be feathers, frills, silk, and lace. Everything massed together. After a moment he saw a small face struggling out of them. The look on that face struck him as either scared or sick. Then, glancing toward Mrs. Grantham, he saw another look entirely.

It was late that evening before he talked with Miss Banker. "You were right—that *was* it," she said. "She did the only thing that, on such short notice, she *could* do. She took the poor thing to the dressmaker."

Sutton buried his face in his hands. "And, oh, the face—the face!" he said.

"Which one?" Miss Banker asked.

"Why, whichever face one looks at," he replied, miserably.

"Ah, but May Grantham looks quite wonderful. She's turned herself out—"

"With great taste and a sense of effect, don't you think?" Sutton showed that he had seen everything.

"She *has* the sense of effect," Miss Banker said. "But what sense of effect is shown in Lady Gwyther's clothes? Everybody's overwhelmed. Here, you know, that sort of mistake is serious. The poor creature is lost!"

"Lost?" he said.

"The first impression is so important. And now it has been made! She will never be able to unmake it."

"But the face—the face!" Sutton said.

"May's?"

"The little girl's. It's so sad. She has begun to see—though she can barely make it out—what has been done to her. She's even worse this evening than she was at tea. My word! Did you see what she was wearing at dinner! Yes, it has dawned on her! She *knows*."

"She should have known before!" said Miss Banker.

"No. She wouldn't in that case have been so beautiful."

"Beautiful?" cried Miss Banker. "But she's overloaded like a monkey in a show!"

"But the *face*! How it goes to the heart! That's what makes it all so horrible!"

"You seem to take it hard," said Miss Banker.

Lord Gwyther had just started to walk over to them. To avoid him, Sutton stepped toward a door that was close at hand. "So hard that I shall be off tomorrow," he said.

"And not see the rest?" she called after him.

He had already gone, though. Lord Gwyther, arriving, took up her question. "The rest of what?"

Miss Banker looked him straight in the eye. "Of Mrs. Grantham's clothes."

Thinking About
the Stories

The Beast in the Jungle

1. Many stories are meant to teach a lesson of some kind. Is the author trying to make a point in this story? What is it?

2. Are there friends or enemies in this story? Who are they? What forces do you think keep the friends together or the enemies apart?

3. Some stories are packed with action. In other stories, the key events take place in the minds of the characters. Is this story told more through the characters' thoughts and feelings? Or is it told more through their outward actions?

The Two Faces

1. Can you think of another good title for this story?

2. Is there a character in this story who makes you think of yourself or someone you know? What did the character say or do to make you think that?

3. Which character in this story do you most admire? Why? Which character do you like the least? Why?